(MIDLE) PF
OUR ROAD
RD WOKING
SURREY GU22 8SP

D0191049

Vampire School

Monster Chef

For Theo and Tara
P.B.
To my Big Brother
C.H.

First published in Great Britain in 2012
by Boxer Books Limited.

www.boxerbooks.com

Based on an original idea by Chris Harrison
Text copyright © 2012 Peter Bently
Illustrations copyright © 2012 Chris Harrison

The rights of Peter Bently to be identified as the author and
Chris Harrison as the illustrator of this work have been asserted by them
in accordance with the Copyright, Designs and Patents Act, 1988.

All rights reserved, including the right of reproduction in whole or in part
in any form. A catalogue record for this book is available from
the British Library.

The illustrations were prepared using biro and watercolour paints.
The text is set in Blackmoor Plain and Adobe Caslon.

ISBN 978-1-907967-27-6

3 5 7 9 10 8 6 4 2

Printed in Great Britain

All of our papers are sourced from managed forests and renewable resources.

Vampire School
Monster Chef

Written by Peter Bently
Illustrated by Chris Harrison

Boxer Books

Contents

Chapter 1
Something Cooking

'Breakfast's ready!' called Lee Price's mum as she opened the door to his bedroom. 'I hope you're all out of bed.'

Mrs Price opened the curtains and saw four bats dangling from the window.

'Ah, there you all are,' she

smiled. 'What are you up to?'

'Nothing, Mum,' said one of the bats. 'Just hanging out.'

'Well, hurry up and change,' said Mum. 'You don't want to be late on your big night, Lee.'

With a soft POP! POP! POP! the bats changed into three children – Lee Price and his best friends, Billy Pratt and Bella Williams.

They
were all
in the
same
class at
St Orlok's

Primary School for young
vampires. The fourth bat was
their friend Boris, a real bat
who lived in the school clock
tower. Billy, Bella and Boris
had been staying at Lee's
house for a Creepover.

'Lee, have you decided what

you're cooking in the contest?'
asked Mum during breakfast.

'Yes,' said Lee, gulping down
a mouthful of Dredded Wheat.
'I'm going to try that recipe
for Batatouille you gave me.'

That night Lee was
representing St Orlok's in the
annual Inter-Ghouls Junior
Monster Chef Competition,

against a werewolf from
Chaney Street First School
and a mummy from Pyramid
Primary. This year it was St
Orlok's turn to hold
the contest.

Lee's class had held its own
cooking competition to choose

who would
represent the
vampires. Lee
was amazed
when Miss
Batula, the
cookery
teacher, had
declared his

Dracaroni Cheese the winner.

'I'm a rubbish cook,' said
Lee. 'I only won because
Miss Batula happens to like
burnt cheese and crunchy
pasta. Billy's Freak Salad was

the best dish by far. It was
a shame Big Herb scoffed it
before the judging!'

'Thanks,' said Billy. 'But I'm
sure you'll win tonight, Lee.'

'I doubt it,' said Lee. 'The
mummies have won five years
running.'

'Yeah,' sighed Bella. 'They reckon they've got the contest all wrapped up.'

'Nonsense!' said Mum. 'Our family have always been good cooks. It's in the blood.'

Chapter 2
Pressure Spooker

After breakfast Lee, Billy and Bella turned into bats again and headed for school with Boris. On the way they met Lee's friend Ollie Talbot, who was on his way to Chaney Street. It was a full moon that night and Ollie was in werewolf form.

'Hi Ollie,' squeaked Lee.
'Coming to the cooking
contest?'

'You bet!' said Ollie,
scratching his ear with his
back paw. 'The whole of our
Year Six is coming to watch.'

'Great!' said Lee nervously.
'So I'll make a right ghoul of
myself in front of two schools!'

'No you won't,' chuckled
Billy. 'It's three schools.
Pyramid Primary are coming
as well, remember!'

'And all my bat friends will
be there,' said Boris. 'I told
them you're going to win!'

'Brilliant,' groaned Lee.

'That's really cheered me up!'

'That's nothing,' said Ollie. 'Guess who's cooking for Chaney Street? Robbie Growler!'

'Oh no!' gasped Lee. 'Not Growler the Fouler!'

The vampires had come across Growler before. He was a big bully and an even bigger cheat.

'Yup,' said Ollie. 'He must have cheated in the qualifier, but no one saw him.'

'How do you know he cheated?' asked Lee.

'Well, everyone's dish was ruined in some weird way,' said Ollie. 'Someone slipped some slugs into my Screech Melba.

Mrs Ripping, our cookery teacher, only realised when she'd swallowed half a slug.'

'Eeeee-uuuuuwwwww!' chorused the bats.

'Growler's was the only dish that wasn't spoiled,' said Ollie. 'So he's in the contest tonight – and all he made was a Boiled Egg!'

'Oh well,' sighed Lee. 'Thanks for the warning, Ollie. Now I know I definitely don't stand a chance!'

The four bats said goodbye to Ollie at the corner of

Chaney Street.
When they got
to St Orlok's,
Lee, Billy and
Bella turned

into vampires and Boris
flapped off home
to the clock tower.
'See you later,
Lee,' he squeaked.
'Good luck in the
competition!'
The young
vampires got to
the classroom and

sat together at the same table.

'Hello everyone,' said their teacher, Miss Gargoyle. 'As you know, tonight is the night of the Inter-Ghouls Junior Monster Chef Competition. The contest takes place after break, down in the Cookery

Crypt. We're all going to be there to see Lee win!'

The class erupted into applause and cries of 'Yay!' and 'Lee rocks!'

'Cheers,' said Lee with a faint smile. 'No pressure, then.'

At that moment the head teacher, Mrs Garlick, rushed in.

'Good evening!' she declared breathlessly. 'I have just heard some exciting news. The winner of tonight's contest will receive a free meal in The Fat Bat!'

'Isn't that the new restaurant run by that chef off the TV?' asked Lee.

'That's right,' said Mrs Garlick. 'The food there is superb. I hear they do a particularly good Coq au Fang. Anyway, I must go and check that everything is ready for the contest. Good luck, Lee. I'm expecting you to win!'

'Thanks,' said Lee glumly. 'I'll try.'

'But you must!' said Mrs Garlick. 'Vampire honour is at stake!'

Chapter 3
Trouble Brewing

When the bell went for break, Lee, Bella and Billy headed for the Cookery Crypt. As they were crossing the playground a line of bats darted down from the clock tower.

It was Boris and his friends.

'Good luck, Lee,' said Boris. 'Vampires rule! Even if they're not real bats!'

'Cheers, Boris,' sighed Lee.

Just then, a bus pulled into the school car park. On the front of the minibus it said

PYRAMID
PRIMARY
SCHOOL.

'Here come the mummies!' said Billy.

The vampires watched as a troop of mummies got out of the bus. Their teacher came over to them with one of the girl mummies.

'Hello!' said the teacher cheerily. 'I'm Sandy Tomb, the cookery teacher from Pyramid Primary. Now, where's Miss Batula?'

'She's already down in the Cookery Crypt,' said Lee.

'Splendid!' guffawed the mummy. 'I'll just go and say how sorry I am that St Orlok's is going to lose – again!'

Sandy Tomb disappeared down into the Cookery Crypt, leaving the vampires gawping.

'Sorry about Mr Tomb,' said the girl mummy. 'His boasting just makes me feel more nervous. I don't think I'm going to win at all!'

'Me neither!' said Lee. 'I'm Lee, by the way. I'm cooking for St Orlok's.'

'I'm Cleo,' said the mummy, pointing at her name badge.

Just then, another bus pulled into the school car park.

'It's the werewolves,' said Bella. 'Look, there's Ollie!'

The vampires waved at Ollie, who waved back. Then a beefy werewolf with a big rucksack

pushed roughly past him and
got off the bus.

'Yikes! And here comes
Growler!' said Billy.

'N-no shoving n-now, b-boys!' said a nervous-looking grown-up werewolf. 'Let's all be on our b-best b-behaviour!'

'Yes, Mrs Ripping,' said Growler. But as soon as she wasn't looking he barged his way through the mummies towards the Cookery Crypt.

'Outta my way,

deadbeats!' he snarled, walloping Cleo with his rucksack. 'Make way for the winner, hur-hur-hur!'

'Hey! Watch where you're going!' said Cleo.

Growler stopped and glared at her.

'Dear me,' he said. 'You look a little tense. I think you need to unwind, hur-hur!'

Growler grabbed the end of Cleo's bandages, gave a great yank and spun her round and round like a top.

'Help! I'm unravelling!' cried Cleo, as Growler ran cackling down the steps into the crypt.

Lee, Billy and Bella helped Cleo to put her bandages back on.

'Rotten bully,' said Bella.

'Thanks,' said Cleo. 'And I'd like to know what he's got in that rucksack!'

'True,' said Lee. 'All our cooking ingredients are already in the Cookery Crypt. Maybe he's up to something!'

Chapter 4
Mummy Mayhem

The huge Cookery Crypt was where the young vampires normally had their Cooking Without Garlic lessons. But tonight most of the worktops had been replaced with rows of chairs for the audience. When everyone was seated Mrs Garlick stood up.

'Ahem! Good evening
and welcome to the Inter-
Ghouls Junior Monster Chef
Competition,' she chirped.
'There will be two rounds to
the contest. In Round One,
the contestants will make a
savoury dish. In Round Two,
they will make a pudding.

Mr Tomb, Mrs Ripping and our own Miss Batula are the judges. They will give marks out of ten for each dish. Now, please welcome our contestants!'

There was a roar of applause as Lee, Cleo and Robbie got up and went to their benches.

'Good luck!' called Bella and Billy as Lee went past them.

'Cheers,' said Lee. 'I'll need it!'

Mrs Garlick held up a stopwatch.

'Let Round One begin,' she trilled. 'You have forty-five minutes starting from NOW!'

She sat down amid another burst of applause.

Lee began to chop vegetables

for his Batatouille. At the next bench, Cleo started slicing an onion for her Shriek and Potato soup. Suddenly, a row

of girl mummies stood up.

'Oh no!' said Cleo. 'Mr Tomb has brought the cheerleaders!'

The mummies started doing
a funny sideways dance and
chanting:

'Two–Four–Six–Eight,
Who do we appreciate?
If you fancy something
yummy,

Let a mummy fill your
tummy!

Give us a C and an L-E-O,
Cleo! Cleo! Way to go!'

• • •

'That is SO embarrassing!'
said Cleo. Tears were pouring
down her face.

'Don't be upset,' said Lee.

'They're not that bad.'

'Oh, I'm not
crying,'
grinned
Cleo. 'It's
this onion.'

Half an hour later, Mrs Garlick declared, 'Ten minutes to go!' and the cheerleaders started up again. They had just got to –

'If you fancy something yummy... '
 – when an egg suddenly flew across the room and – KERSPLAT! – landed on the chief cheerleader!

'Arrgghh!'

The cheerleader lost her balance and went flying into the mummy next to her, who tumbled into the next mummy – until the cheerleaders were a tangled heap of arms, legs and bandages.

'Who threw that egg?'

demanded Mr Tomb.

'It was him!' The chief cheerleader pointed at Growler. 'That hairy-faced horror over there!'

'Whoops!' sniggered Growler. 'It must've slipped out of my hand! Hur-hur!'

'Slipped?' said Mr Tomb. 'If that was an accident I'm a zombie!'

'What's up?' growled Growler. 'Can't you take a yolk? Hur-hur-hur!'

'Now then, Robbie,' said Mrs Ripping. 'Any m-more of that and I shall g-get jolly c-cross! Jolly c-cross indeed!'

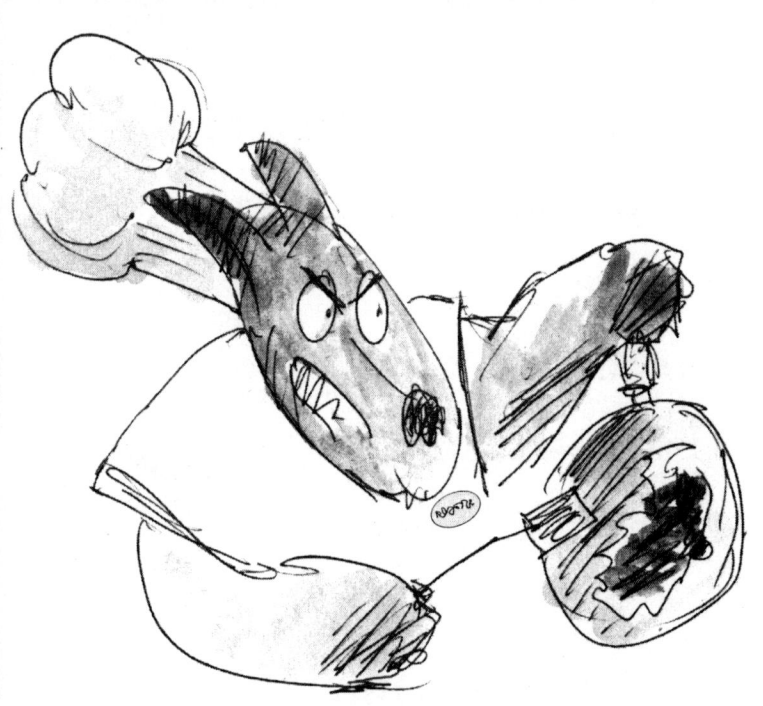

Lee suddenly smelled smoke.

'Hey, Robbie,' he said. 'Your
Strangled Egg is burning!'

Growler stopped smirking.

'Drat!' he said, scraping
burnt bits of egg out of the pan.

'Serves him right,' whispered
Cleo.

Just at that moment Mrs
Garlick checked
her watch and
announced,
'Time's up!'

The three cookery
teachers gave Lee eight out of
ten for his Batatouille. Cleo
also got eight points for her

Shriek and Potato Soup.
But Robbie received zero for
his burnt Strangled Egg on
Toast.

'There will now be a break
for lunch!' declared Mrs
Garlick. 'We shall return in
one hour for Round Two of the
competition. No one is allowed
in the Cookery
Crypt during
the break!'

Chapter 5
Crypt Capers

'So far, so good,' said Lee during lunch.

'Yeah,' said Cleo. 'At least we're both ahead of Growler.'

'Talking of Growler, where is he?' said Lee. 'I can't see him anywhere.'

'Who knows?' said Cleo.

'Wait here,' said Boris. 'I'll go and check.'

Boris fluttered off and did a quick tour of the playground. He soon spotted Growler skulking in the bushes near the school Sick Bay. Then he watched as Growler sneaked back into the Cookery Crypt.

'No one's allowed there during lunch,' thought Boris. 'Growler's definitely up to no good!'

He spotted a tiny window, just above ground level. It was open just far enough for Boris to squeeze through into the Crypt.

Growler was in the corner with his back to Boris. He was unpacking something from his rucksack.

'Hur-hur!' sniggered Growler. 'If those stupid ghouls think they're going to win they're in for a nasty surprise!'

'Lee was right!' thought Boris. 'Growler's going to cheat! But how can I prove it?'

He looked around the kitchen and noticed Growler's mobile phone on a bench.

'Aha!' thought Boris. 'I wonder...'

• • •

Five minutes later, Boris was heading back to the window when the doorknob started to rattle. Someone was coming into the Cookery Crypt!

'Nng!' grunted a voice. 'Zis pesky door is stiff!'

'Yikes!'
thought Boris.
'It's old Gore!'
Mr Eric Gore
was the school zombie
caretaker. He was the world's
biggest moaner and he hated
vampires.

Boris darted
sideways into
a cupboard
and crouched
behind a
bottle of
ketchup.

Growler also heard the door and hastily grabbed his rucksack.

'Uh-oh,' he smirked. 'Time to go! Now where's my phone? Never mind, I'll find it later. After I've won! And no one will ever know I cheated! Hur-hur!'

Growler hid behind the door just as old Gore burst

in carrying a large net. He
looked around suspiciously.

'I'm sure I heard a rat in
here!' he groaned. 'No vonder!
All zese bits of food everyvere.
Vot a mess! Zose pesky
vampires and zeir shtupid
cookery contest!'

Old Gore started prowling
around the Crypt.

'Come out, little ratties!' he
gurgled. 'Come to your nice
Uncle Eric!'

Then he spied the window
that Boris had slipped
through.

'Aha! Maybe you got in here, eh?' he grunted. 'Pesky vampires! Always leaving sings open!'

Gore went over to the window and pulled it shut.

'Bother!' thought Boris. 'That was my escape route!'

While Gore was closing the window, Growler sneaked out from behind the door and silently crept out of the Crypt.

'That's the only
way out,' thought Boris.
'I'll have to risk it!'

But then Gore suddenly turned and headed straight for Boris's hiding place!

'Typical!' Gore grouched. 'Some shtupid vampire has left zis cupboard open too! Ze whole place is rat heaven!'

And before Boris could move, the cupboard door slammed shut and everything went dark.

Chapter 6
Kitchen Chaos

'Has anyone seen Boris?'
wondered Lee, as everyone
headed back to the Crypt for
Round Two. 'He said he was

going to check on Growler.'

'No,' said Billy. 'And Growler's over there.'

'Maybe he wasn't up to anything, after all,' said Cleo.

'Maybe,' said Lee. 'But why hasn't Boris come back?'

It seemed weird. Boris was keen to see the contest, so what could have held him up?

Lee was still thinking about it as he got to his bench in the Crypt for Round Two. In this round, the three contestants had to make something sweet.

Mum had given Lee a recipe for Upside-Down Tart. Cleo was making a Coffin-and-Walnut Cake. Growler was baking Apple Grumble.

'Has anyone seen the sugar?' asked Lee.

To Lee's surprise, Growler politely handed it to him.

'Er, thanks,' said Lee.

'No problem,' smiled Growler. 'My pleasure.'

Lee measured out the sugar and added it to his tart mix. Meanwhile, Cleo was hunting for the walnuts for her cake.

'Here,' said Growler, passing the jar.

'Oh thanks, Gr— um, Robbie,' said Cleo.

'No worries,' grinned Growler.

Cleo glanced at Lee.

'I can't believe it!'

she whispered. 'Growler's actually being nice!'

'I know,' said Lee. 'Spooky, isn't it?'

Everything else went smoothly. By the time Mrs Garlick called, 'Time's up!' all three puddings were out of the oven. 'Well, as they say, the proof of the pudding is in the eating,' declared Mrs Garlick. 'So our judges will now try the dishes.'

They tried Growler's Apple
Grumble first.

'T-tasty!' beamed
Mrs Ripping.

'Delicious!' nodded
Miss Batula.

'Yum!' agreed Mr Tomb.

Next, Mrs Garlick cut three

slices of Lee's Upside-Down Tart and gave one to each of the judges.

They took a bite. They smiled. They chewed. They smiled a little less. They chewed more slowly. Then

suddenly – they all spat out
the cake!

'It's horrible!' spluttered
Miss Batula.

'D-disgusting!' coughed Mrs
Ripping.

'It's – it's got SALT in it
instead of SUGAR!'
blurted Mr Tomb.

They all stared
at Lee.

'No way!' he said,
horrified. 'There
must be some
mistake.'

Lee dipped his finger into the bag of sugar and tasted it. Mr Tomb was right. The bag was full of salt! Lee glared at Growler.

'Dear me,' smiled Growler innocently. 'However could that have happened?'

The judges moved on to Cleo's Coffin-and-Walnut Cake. They each took

a mouthful, chewed,
swallowed and then –

'Yuuuurcchh!'

'Uggghh!'

'Eeeeuuuuuuuuw!'

'My word!' said Mrs Garlick.
'What is it this time? Salt
instead of sugar again?'

'No!' said Miss Batula. 'It's
the walnuts!'

'They've gone all chewy!'
said Mrs Ripping.

'And they taste
like poo!'
said Mr
Tomb
 Mrs
Garlick
peered
into the
jar.

'Well, they look all
right...'

Just then, a little bald
vampire with round glasses
popped his head around

the door of the Crypt. It was Dr Chestikoff, the school doctor.

'Sorry to interrupt,' said Dr Chestikoff. 'I've been looking everywhere for... ah! There they are!'

He strode to Cleo's bench and picked up the jar of walnuts.

'I wouldn't bother with those walnuts if I were you,' said Mrs Garlick.'

'Walnuts? These aren't walnuts,' said Dr Chestikoff. 'They're Pickled Rat Brains. A most excellent laxative! Works instantly! Goodnight!'

As Dr Chestikoff pottered back to the Sick Bay, he was rather surprised to see Miss

Batula, Mrs Ripping and Mr
Tomb dashing past him into
the staff toilets.

Cleo looked furiously at
Growler.

'Oh dear,' said Growler.
'Wonder how they could have
got there. Hur-hur!'

'Now to the scores,' said

Mrs Garlick, after the three teachers had returned. 'How many points for Cleo's Coffin-and-Walnut Cake?'

'Zero, I'm afraid!' said Miss Batula, who still looked as green as a zombie.

'Nil!' said Mrs Ripping.

'Nothing!' said Mr Tomb.

'Very well,' said Mrs Garlick. 'So Cleo finishes on eight

points! Will you now give us the scores for Lee's Upside-Down Tart?'

'Also zero!' said Miss Batula.

'Diddly-squat!' said Mrs Ripping.

'Zilcheroony!' agreed Mr Tomb.

'So Lee also finishes on eight points!' said Mrs Garlick. 'And finally, please give us the scores for Robbie's Apple

Grumble!'

'It was quite delicious,' said Mr Tomb. 'Nine out of ten!'

'Robbie finishes the contest on nine points,' said Mrs Garlick. 'I therefore declare Robbie Growler the winner! Congratulations on becoming the new Junior Monster Chef!'

The audience cheered – but

there were also a
few moans and
hisses.

Billy, Bella
and Ollie went
over to Lee
and Cleo.

'Bad luck,' said
Bella. 'Though I don't think
luck had much to do with it.'

'Too right,' said Ollie. 'We
all saw Growler giving Lee
the salt and Cleo the jar of
rat brains.'

'But we can't prove

anything,' said Lee gloomily.

'Now,' said Mrs Garlick. 'It is time to present the prize. It's in an envelope in this cupboard.'

She opened the cupboard – and out flew Boris the bat!

'Boris!' said Lee in surprise. 'So that's where you've been! What on earth were you doing in there?'

'Long story,' said Boris. 'The main thing is Growler can't win. He cheated!'

Everyone gasped.

'That is a very s-serious accusation,' said Mrs Ripping.

'I demand an explanation!' said Mrs Garlick.

'I saw Growler sneaking in here during the break,' said Boris. 'I followed him and saw him switching the sugar and the walnuts!'

'But h-how can you prove it?' said Mrs Ripping.

'He can't!' snarled Growler.

'He's talking rubbish!'

Boris ignored him.

'I spotted Growler's mobile,' he said. 'I wanted to call a teacher so they could catch him red-handed. But Growler would have heard me, so I didn't.'

'Hur-hur!' sneered Growler. 'See! He can't prove anything!'

'That's what you think,' grinned Boris. 'I didn't use the phone to call anyone. But I did turn on the phone camera. It should have filmed everything! It's behind that bag of potatoes.'

Growler tried to grab his mobile – but Mrs Garlick reached it first.

'Not so fast!' she said sharply. 'Let's see what we've got here, shall we?'

Mrs Garlick, Miss Batula, Mr Tomb and Mrs Ripping all gathered round

Growler's phone. The screen
was tiny but clear enough to
see.

They watched open-mouthed
as the video showed Growler
tipping the sugar down the
sink and filling up the bag
from a box marked SALT.

Then he took a large jar labelled PICKLED RAT BRAINS out of his rucksack.

'Hur-hur!' they heard him say, as he peeled off the label. 'I'll put these back in the Sick Bay later and no one will ever know!'

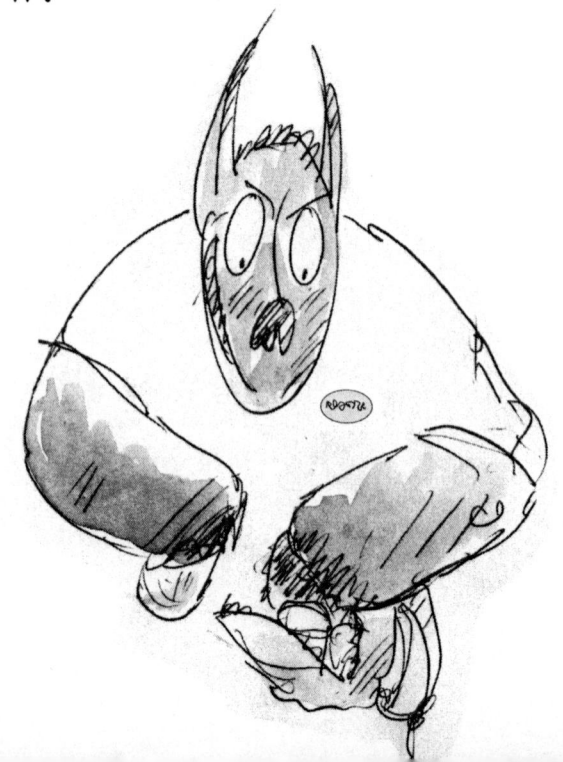

Finally, the teachers watched Growler unwrap a perfect ready-made Apple Grumble and slide it into the oven.

'There,' said Growler on the video. 'I'll put my own rubbish Apple Grumble into the oven, but the Apple Grumble I take out will be this one! Lucky there's a nice bakery on the way to school, hur-hur.'

Mrs Garlick switched off the phone. Everyone stared at Growler.

'Um, I can explain

everything,' he grinned sheepishly.

'You c-certainly can,' said Mrs Ripping. 'You can explain it to Mrs Savage in her office, first thing tomorrow night!'

Growler's grin disappeared. Mrs Savage was the head of Chaney Street school.

Mrs Garlick turned to the audience.

'Well, I think we are all

agreed that Robbie Growler
must be disqualified,' she
said. 'Lee and Cleo have eight
points each, so
I declare them
joint winners
of this year's
Junior Monster
Chef!'

There was a loud burst of
applause from all the children
as Mrs Garlick presented the
prize to Lee and Cleo.

'Well done, you two!' said Billy and Bella.

'And well done, Boris,' said Ollie. 'For proving that Growler cheated!'

'Too right,' said Lee. 'You can come with us to The Fat Bat when we go for our free meal.'

'Please come,' said Cleo.
'You deserve it!'

'Thanks, I'd love to!' beamed
Boris. 'Do you think they
serve fresh bluebottles?'

The
End

MORE
FANGTASTIC

Vampire School titles to enjoy